THE MUDDY SEASON

THE MUDDY SEASON

Matthew Raymond

Black Lawrence Press

Black
Lawrence
Press

www.blacklawrence.com

Executive Editor: Diane Goettel
Chapbook Editor: Kit Frick
Book and cover design: Amy Freels

Copyright © Matthew Raymond 2016
ISBN: 978-1-62557-963-8

Published 2016 by Black Lawrence Press.
Printed in the United States.

I

She was born in the muddy season, with the rain coming steadily down and the villagers standing at the window looking in. Pulling her blue and wet from her mother and saying quietly, Life is suffering, the midwife smacked her until she cried, then dried her and wrapped her and laid her in her mother's arms. Thanks be to God, the villagers said, and they made the movement of their hands over their hearts which was a gesture of code between the heavens and their souls, a sort of selfblessing, for they were endowed with that capacity. Then they stepped out from under the eaves and went back to the fields, working as they did all through the wet summers.

Her mother, weak from the labor, wasn't so much holding her newborn child in her arms as she was tolerating its weight against her bosom and biceps. She seemed in a daze, as if asleep, yet staring out the open window at the blur of quiet rain, at the heavy clouds which eased themselves against the hills, the hills seeming to wait patiently, to accept everything that came down upon them. The first thing her mother did after resting in that glaze-eyed exhaustion was cry.

Or rather: They were born in the muddy season, with the rain coming down steadily and the villagers standing at the window looking in and the government agent sitting under the front awning in his strange outfit that removed all contour from his body. He appeared not to hear the cries of the labor, the moaning, the sharp native cursing, but only looked calmly out over the wet land.

Pulling first her sister and then her from their sweating, heaving mother, the first midwife said under her breath, Life is suffering, and smacked them each one until they cried. Then the second midwife dried them each one and laid them in the arms of their mother. The mother made no move to hold her babies. She tried to ignore their gentle bare weight against her bosom and biceps, her eyes staring out the window of the one room house at the thick clouds pushing down on the hills, which were so patient and accepting of the rain, though it was heavier that year and constant with the promise of floods.

The villagers standing at the window made the sign over their hearts which was their code of faith between the heavens and their hearts, a gesture which was made as often and with as much thought as turning their heads to spit. They said, Thanks be to God, and turned and stepped out from under the eaves and went back to the fields where they worked all day every summer regardless of the weather, heavy rain or scorching sun. They did not look at the government agent on the porch, and he did not look at them. Out by the road was the agent's truck, in the back of which soldiers sat smoking cigarettes and playing cards.

When the cries of the mother had stopped and the new cries began, the agent stood up. He passed his hand over the front of his shirt as if to smooth any wrinkle, though there was no wrinkle to smooth. Then, abruptly, he stopped, turned his head ever so slightly. Was it two babies that he heard? He listened a moment. Yes, he realized, two. He took his leather folder from the floor where it leaned against a chair leg and set it on the chair and searched through it until he found the papers he needed and pulled them out. He also took out a small black book and flipped through it a moment. Reading something in the tiny lettering, he nodded and then put the book back in the folder.

Or: They were born in the muddy season and both cried as if they knew their fate or as if they couldn't bear the trauma of the world now theirs. The afterbirth spilled out a moment later onto the packed mud floor just as the government agent eased open the door and stood there wide-eyed as if it were his first time away from the capital. You wait, the first midwife said sternly, holding her hand up to him. He looked guilty already but tried to maintain an air of authority, framed in the doorway like a painting from some other age, some other world. The State is waiting, he said. But the glaring eyes of the midwife were no match for his and he looked as if he might cry at any moment. Then he composed himself, ignored any upsurge in his heart and stomach, and came in and laid his leather folder on the rough wooden table.

The second midwife, a mere girl, had the placenta in a pail and she took it to the stove where she dumped it into a steaming pot of dark water along with a bowl of leaves which had been on the shelf above the stove. The agent watched, the first midwife still glaring at him. He was a pale thin man who, like most of those from the capital, seemed unable to conceive of wearing anything but dark clothing, preferably solid black, although a dark blue was sometimes worn. The midwife had seen this one before. She kept her eyes hard on him, not moving, her hands still wet from the birth. The agent glared back at her and for a moment the room was so still that it seemed no one was in it save for the crying babies. When he could hold her gaze no longer, he stepped to the door and, producing a whistle from somewhere on his person, he put it to his lips and blew a short shrill note. A moment later three soldiers came up under the awning with their complicated looking carbines held crosswise before them. One came inside and stood by the door, the other two stayed out. The midwife did not alter her stance in the slightest. She was a thick sturdy woman. Just keep quiet, the agent said, not looking at her but arranging his papers on the table as he spoke. You know you'll be paid. He took a pen from the breast pocket of his uniform and filled in portions of the forms. And anyway, he added, in the case of twins, it's only the firstborn we acquire. She can keep the other one.

I'll forgo my payment if you say they both died in the birth, the midwife said. It was an arrangement that had worked in the past, though rarely.

They'll want to see bodies, the agent said.

The villagers can offer you something. We can—

Listen, the agent said, looking up from his papers and out the window, I can't help you. It's too risky, the State would reduce me at the very least. He sighed. You people should know better. Then he looked at the midwife and held out the pen. Sign, he said.

She took the pen, snatching it almost, almost breaking it, and nearly broken herself, and yet she leaned over the papers in the soft light of the window and signed. When she stood up, her bloody hands had left the papers wet and stained. The agent seemed to accept this.

But it was the muddy season and muddier than any previous year in memory. Her sister did come out first, screaming and blue into the midwife's clean strong hands, and though by her crying she seemed to understand it already, still the midwife uttered the saying as she slapped her: Life is suffering. There was more to say during a birth, custom decreed, but she had no time because the government agent had come and had been waiting on the porch since before dawn. He hadn't asked for food or drink, only sat quietly all morning under the awning while it rained, once in a while going to have a cigarette with the troops in the truck parked on the road.

Quickly she handed the firstborn to the second midwife and made ready for the next. When she and her sister were both dry and crying less furiously, the second midwife, a mere girl, stood holding her sister, the firstborn, and looking plaintively at the head midwife who held her, the secondborn. Which one? the girl said. My God, what difference does it make? the older woman said, her voice betraying her anger at having to be the one to make such a choice. Without pausing she took the one she held to the window and handed it to one of the women who was standing outside with the others. She was a large woman and when she'd slung the infant into the shawl that was tied over her shoulder and let it hang down under her heavy arm, the tiny thing was barely discernible among the folds of her clothing and the mounds of her flesh. All those standing at the window made the sign over their hearts which was a gesture to God and a sort of selfblessing, and as they turned and stepped out from under the eaves and into the rain, they began to sing. It was a song of birth that should have been joyful, but they were not singing to celebrate this birth, only to conceal it, for the infant was crying this whole time. They walked huddled in a group so as to further disguise any hint of the child among them, and they remained grave as they went away from the house toward the fields, looking at each other from the corners of their narrow eyes, their voices going up with the melody and down. All was well but that the skinny dog with lesions visible on its skin where the hair had fallen out barked at them and at the smell of new life that issued from them, which to it was like the smell of meat. It stood away from the house and away from the crowd and wouldn't go near either, yet neither would it cease its yapping.

One man broke away from the others and went toward the dog with his hoe in his hand. The dog seemed to cower but still went on barking until the man, once close enough, gave it a swift kick in the jaw. There was a yelp and a good solid pop as its mouth clapped shut and the agent looked up when he heard it. He'd been listening to the song, which wasn't in his language, and wondering at the sounds, which sounded like animal sounds to him yet which the villagers took for words. He looked up and saw only the peasant man standing in the rain looking at him while the dog skulked away toward the chicken pens at the edge of the fields.

I heard two, the agent said when he entered the one-room house. There were two.

You're insane, the midwife said, her eyes hard on him. She faced him squarely and her accent in the official tongue gave the words a harsh sound.

The agent surveyed the room. The new mother lay wilted in the bed, which stood opposite the window and beside the stove, and the

newborn was in her arms and crying. The second midwife stood at
the stove stirring a steaming pot, her back to the room. She was just
a girl, her figure slight but coming into its fullness, and when she
turned her head to look over her shoulder at the room, the agent
caught the tiny sharp light in the dark of her eyes. The rich aroma
from the pot came into his nostrils and he realized he was hungry.

He turned to the first midwife and was about to issue an
authoritative declaration, but she immediately cut him off. Just do
your job, she said.

Flustered, he set his papers on the table and had the midwife
sign and had the second midwife sign in lieu of the mother, who
only stared dull-eyed out the window.

Who is the father? the agent asked.

There is none.

What do you mean?

I mean there is no father.

Don't tell me the woman has had intercourse with God. I've
heard it too many times. The State has heard it too many times. It
won't accept such an answer. Who is the father?

The midwife glared at him. He's dead.

She was obviously lying and all the agent had to do to prove
it was, once he got back to the Municipal Palace, look up the
death reports for that district. Then he could file a complaint and
repercussions would follow. But that would also mean several more
trips out to this dirty insect-infested place, and he did not want that.

He's dead, the midwife said flatly.

Just give me a name. It doesn't matter who, anyone, so long as
it's male and he lives in this district.

The midwife didn't say anything.

He doesn't even need to live in this district, it just makes things easier if he does.

She looked at him with her dark eyes.

Dead men tend to require more paperwork, and more fees. Then the agent said the native word for taxes. The death will have to be verified. Just give me any name.

She gave him a very common name and he scribbled it down on the appropriate forms. The smell of the pot on the stove was thick in the room and his stomach tightened with hunger. But he wouldn't eat their cooking, the State advised against it.

The newborn still cried. The agent went to the door and blew a small shrill whistle, one quick note, and a moment later three soldiers came in. He only had to nod at them and they knew what to do. Two of them stood by the door holding their carbines crosswise before them while the third shouldered his and went to the bedside. As soon as the soldier took the baby up from the mother, it stopped its crying. The soldier was startled by the silence. He held the infant up in his big pale hands like a sack of rice and it did not cry though it writhed in the rough woolen blanket. The soldier looked at the agent, who seemed struck dumb as well, and immediately threw his hand toward the door, revoking any hesitation anywhere, in the soldier or in himself. The soldier held the child before him as if it were diseased and went out of the door and was gone.

All the while, the mother stared out the window at the hills blurred by the rain and at the clouds pressing against them. The hills seemed to accept everything that came down. Whatever it was, however much, it would be accommodated. The hills knew nothing of flooding, for flooding was only a name the villagers gave to the water when it wasted their crops, when it came into their houses and softened their dirt floors.

Later, when her only child grew older and full of questions, the mother would tell her nothing more than that she had been born in the muddy season and that the midwife had uttered the saying and slapped her until she cried and became a part of this great world.

The truck had come down the road through the dense foliage just before dawn and stopped where the road ended, by the low stone buildings that served as the provincial outpost for the State. The engine was shut off and the truck sat there in the dark in silence. With the first bare light of dawn the driver's elbow in green fatigues could be seen resting on the windowsill, smoke from his cigarette drifting out the window and mingling with the mist. A soldier jumped out of the back of the truck in the madrugal light, took a few steps away, groped at his pants and stood pissing in the road.

Soon the passenger door opened and the agent climbed down and his shiny boots sank ankle deep in the mud. He walked around the truck to the nearest of the buildings holding his leather folder in his left hand and bracing a thermos under that same thin arm. Putting a key into the lock he tried to turn it but it would not and he worked at it but it didn't move. He put his shoulder against the door and leaned heavily but his feet slid in the mud and he almost fell, catching himself on the doorknob and dropping the thermos. Without being asked the soldier who sat behind the wheel jumped down from the truck and came to the door. After a few seconds of working at the lock he stood back and kicked the door in. The agent scolded him, but the soldier just held up his hands and shrugged and walked back to the truck.

The office smelled of mold and dampness and was bare save for a large desk and a filing cabinet behind. The agent set his things on the desk and unlocked the top drawer and took out a bound logbook. He logged his name, number, the date, the time, and the purpose of his visit. Then he unscrewed the lid of his thermos, which served as a cup, and he poured coffee into it and sat back and lit a cigarette.

Looking out the window, still and quiet the cool gray dawn, he saw a girl go by in the road carrying a bucket and he got up and went out and stopped her. He asked her where the woman who was having the baby lived. The girl pointed to a cluster of huts situated in the mist beyond the stone buildings of the State: native buildings of salvaged clapboard and sheet metal with thatching for roofs. She didn't look at the agent and didn't speak. She was dirty: face, hair, clothes, all dirty. When she went off down the road, she glanced back quickly and then, seeing the agent's eyes still on her, turned and ran, the bucket swinging and rattling against her leg.

The agent went back in and sat at the desk drinking his coffee and reading the regulation book while he waited.

By full morning he'd seen several people go by in the road, some looking in the door of the office as they went, others appearing not to even notice the huge army truck sitting there in front. He took his leather folder and went out and spoke to the driver a moment. Then he set off down the mud track that led to the fields and to the clusters of buildings that were emerging clearer and clearer from the mist. Men and women were already bent over out in the fields and others were coming and going between the huts. Some looked up at him as he went, one or two even nodded, but none smiled.

He stepped under the front overhang of the hut and stopped, listened. He did not speak or understand much of the native tongue of these parts—only what he had to—but he could tell what was happening inside. The labor had begun.

But in fact the regime was not so well organized. The agent and his men, who were not really *his* men, had been in the village for three days before her mother felt her first contraction. In addition to the desk and the filing cabinet, there was also a cot in the office and several old army blankets. The agent kept himself there while the soldiers, nine in all, occupied one of the buildings across the road.

Her mother was alone that first morning the agent came to see her, three days before her first contraction. She did not understand any of the official language and the agent could only cough out a few words in her tongue. He stood in the doorway holding his folder at his side and he moved his mouth strangely as he said, Child. Your child. It will become a ward of the State. Control of the population by means of regulation. Understand? Her mother retorted quickly that there was a will in the world that touched the people but that the people could never touch and when she gives birth God will have it as he wishes. She almost spit the words out she spoke so fast and the agent didn't understand any of it but the word God. He saw her hand move over her heart, which was something the natives did out of some religious habit. He looked at her. He blinked. She was huge with her child and he was glad, for it meant he wouldn't have to wait around too long.

As he went out the door of the hut, a girl was coming toward it. She stepped under the overhang and nodded and made to pass into the house, but he said to her, Do you speak the Tongue? She nodded. He told her to make sure the woman knew what was to happen. The girl said yes and then stood there as if waiting for further instructions or a formal dismissal. The agent, upon looking more closely at her, thought she might be the same girl he'd stopped in the road earlier that morning. She was dark and messy but her lines were soft and her eyes clear and serious, though she wouldn't look directly at him. He stood there looking at her, seemed to be examining her for some hidden thing, or looking at her as if he'd never seen a native before. Finally when he spoke, his tone was quiet and entirely different than the order he'd just given her. He said, I'll need some food. Bring something to the office later.

She nodded and then stepped into the hut and shut the door, before which the agent stood a moment before turning away.

By the end of that first day the villagers knew that the agent and the soldiers were not of the same mind. The agent in his more formal dress seemed to be the one in charge, but that afternoon some of the villagers saw him and the soldier who had driven the truck standing in the middle of the road between the two stone buildings yelling at each other. None of the villagers spoke the official tongue well enough to follow their argument, but the soldier, who was taller and bigger, yelled louder and pointed to his own chest as if speaking of something inside him, and the agent kept his arms folded before him or else held his hands out open as if to say their emptiness and paleness were not his fault.

The girl brought a pot of stew to the office just after dark. She stood in the doorway looking in. The agent lay on the cot with his arm over his eyes and the girl waited until something in the silence made him flinch and he looked up and, seeing her, quickly rose and said, Come in.

She set the pot on the desk and set a large wooden spoon beside it. The agent looked at her as if he could look nowhere else. There was only one lantern on the desk and the side of the girl that was lit seemed to glow in the surrounding dark, her simple wool dress dirty and her dark arms dirty too, but in a way that he thought must be uncleanable and therefore admissible. The dark side of her was as dark as the rest of the room and he could not see it. Her strange rude smell came into his nostrils and he breathed it in.

Will you eat? he said as he went to the desk and turned up the lantern to see her better.

She shook her head.

There was only the desk chair in the room and he pulled it out and set it by her and said in the native tongue, Sit. But she wouldn't, and neither would she meet his eye. Then she said, Some of the villagers are afraid of the soldiers. They are afraid of trouble with them.

No, he said. There will be no trouble.

She looked at the floor.

Sit, he said. But she didn't.

He took the chair and sat and ate the stew, which he guessed was the jungle rodent that was the staple of the native diet.

The girl watched him as he ate. He ate slowly and watched her.

After a time the girl said, I'll come for the pot tomorrow. And before he could stop her, she turned and her darkness disappeared out the door into the rest of the darkness.

The next morning a man came to his office early and said he had to speak to the agent. The agent sat behind the desk and said, So speak. The man said that last night some of the soldiers had gone to the meeting house and taken several bottles of cane liquor without paying. They got very drunk there in the meeting house and there was a fight, which the man insisted was initiated by the soldiers, and now a very old man of the village was incapacitated with a broken rib.

When the agent went into the building across the road, everyone was asleep except one young soldier, just a boy, who was leaning over a sink on the far wall and vomiting. His back was to the agent and he didn't turn around when he answered the agent's questions.

The sergeant and D.B. were drunk, the soldier said.

Well, didn't anybody try to stop them?

We were all drunk. The soldier coughed something up and spit it into the sink.

Tell the sergeant to come and see me when he gets up. The agent went back to his office and sat down on the cot, rubbing his hands together as he stared out the window.

Or did no one come that morning to complain to the agent? The villagers, though they knew the agent and the soldiers were not of the same mind, saw them nonetheless as inseparable. No one came that morning. The agent had gone across the road only to make sure everyone was still there and to talk to the sergeant about what he'd seen the night before and about the note left in his office. Everyone was asleep in the barracks and he looked at them in their cots a moment and then turned and left.

The night before he haayd set his spoon down in the pot of stew and stepped to the doorway to watch where the girl went. He left the door to the office open and followed her at a distance. When she got to the cluster of huts, he stepped off the main track and went behind the houses, jogging ahead so that he was even with her, watching her between the houses until she passed them all and set out across the fields, walking on the mud path between the worked plots. He was left standing behind the meeting house, the last building on the edge of that group of ramshackle squats and the only building with a raised floor. He watched the girl go lightly on her bare feet and disappear into the dark, and even after she disappeared he squinted and thought he might still be seeing her. Then he heard the fight break out inside the meeting house. Chairs scraping along the plank floor, wood cracking, glass shattering. He listened to the sergeant's voice, a barrage of mispronounced curses in the native tongue. The agent crept back to his office. He almost slipped on the note as he stepped through the door, for they had left it right inside, a pile of human shit that was quite fresh and reeking horribly.

The sergeant came in at midmorning the next day in his khakis and undershirt with his sidearm hanging from his belt. He looked tired but was nonetheless daunting with his thick body and pockmarked face. He smoked a cigarette and sat on the agent's cot. The agent looked at him from behind the desk.

Don't get up my ass about it, the sergeant said. Nobody wants to hear it.

The agent looked out the window. It would just make things easier if you and your men had any sense of respect.

The sergeant shook his head. Listen. You know just like I do.

The agent turned to the sergeant, his eyes dull with the gray light of another gray day. I just want to get out of here without getting killed, he said.

Then do your fucking job. The sergeant got up and left.

The second night the girl again brought the pot and it was the same stew and he told her to sit but she wouldn't and he offered her the food that she had brought but she said no. And then he ate and watched her and she watched him. She said she would wait until he was done and then take the pot.

When she left he stepped to the door and watched her go and then stepped out and pulled the door shut and followed her. She went again among the native houses, stopping at one to set the pot on the doorstep, and then she went on through the dark village to the fields and set out across. The agent waited until she was no longer visible. Then he went after her down the path between the plots and toward the dense wall of jungle on the other side.

So the truck had come down the road just before dawn and it stopped there and stayed there all day even though her mother hadn't even had a contraction yet and it wouldn't leave even after some of the villagers had left a shovelful of human shit on the doorstep of the office where the agent kept himself. The soldiers stayed in a building across the road from the office, but none of the villagers would leave fresh dung on that doorstep. There was a villager who went to the office on the morning of the second day to complain about the fight that the soldiers had initiated on the previous night, but when he stepped in the door, which stood wide open, there was no one, only the pile of shit still sitting there. He went back down to the village proper, to a house that stood apart, farthest from the government buildings and apart from their own buildings, and he knocked on the door. The midwife opened it and ushered him in.

They sat at a table and looked out over the fields and the men and women there bent over working.

Your sister is almost ready, the midwife said. A few days.

The man looked out the window. The midwife got up and went to the stove and poured water from a blackened pot into a bowl full of twigs and leaves. She set a plate upside down over the bowl and brought it to the table.

There is something you should know, she said.

The man looked up at her where she stood beside the table. She was an older woman but not frail or ailing.

Twins, the midwife said. She has two inside her.

The man blessed himself. I will tell the others, he said.

The midwife took the plate off of the bowl and poured the contents through a cloth and into a cup and the man sat drinking it.

She was saved. The villagers smuggled her across the fields under the misty clouds that pushed against the hills, took her into the dark jungle, the fat one carrying her in a sling under her arm, the child crying all the while. She took the child through the steaming potent forest, up the hills and down, pushing aside the foliage and trotting past the giant anthill in the clearing and across the open meadow and up the rocky bluff, the trail all back and forth there, and into the cave that they had prepared, the cave they used to store what weapons they could steal or smuggle in and what food they would need for the hard times they were expecting. The cave where they planned their attacks, argued their strategies. The child cried like the light of day was a menace to its being and the old witch doctor bathed it in a bath that had been prepared for it and he spoke many incantations as this child's salvation bespoke a promise to them all that they would one day succeed. Then the young wet nurse took her from the blanket and held her like her own all day long and into the night until finally the child took to the nipple and was silent.

She was saved. The people of her village sang to cover her cries as they walked back to the fields in a cluster, dispersing with their hoes into the plots only to preserve an aspect of normality on that most abnormal of days. The day of her birth. One of them had broken away from the group and went and kicked the dog which had smelled her new smell and was barking wildly. The dog skulked off toward the chicken coop and the man stood there in the rain looking at the agent who sat on the porch while the fat one hurried across the fields with the child slung under her arm. This man stood there as the agent went into the house and was there when the agent came out again and blew his shrill little whistle. He watched as three soldiers came out of the barracks where he'd been afraid to leave a pile of shit to intimidate them and he watched them enter the house and was watching as they came out, one carrying the child before him like a sack of fetid garbage.

This man watching is the brother of the mother of that child and though through careful planning one child has been saved, he can only watch so long before he is compelled to follow the soldiers. He walks toward the barracks where they are headed, where he was afraid to leave a pile of shit to intimidate them. He walks steadily, his hoe held loosely, carefully in one hand, the way he would carry it out in the morning and home in the evening on any other day.

The soldier with the child has gone into the barracks, followed by the other two. They are standing looking at the baby, the one holding it up now, looking at its face and making a noise with his mouth. Some of the others look too, but most want nothing to do with it. It is a long day's drive back to the capital and nobody wants to take care of the thing. The soldier holding the baby and making noises turns when the shadow of the native fills the doorway, the hoe at his side. It is a simple tool for turning the soil. Before a word is said, the man raises it with both hands and swings it, swiftly, deftly, into the baby's soft skull. Blood runs over the soldier's hands and though trained to not flinch at the sight of blood, he cries out, the blood dripping onto the floor and his comrades cursing and chasing the man with the hoe out the door and down the lane away from the fields where he is running. The soldier with the baby momentarily loses his composure, a weak moan leaking out of his stunned face, and one of his comrades urges him to take the bloody fucking thing outside, which he does, and in a futile attempt to rid himself of complicity, he chucks it to the ground where it lies in its blankets in the mud with the fine rain falling gently on it and blood gurgling from its head.

IV

A man can know what rules govern the societies of men. He can study them and memorize them and ponder their machinations. But it will be a long time before he discovers that those rules, those theorems, do not apply to his own life. His life is an original form determined by structures and forces within himself, which he can never fully know. To begin with, he is afraid of these forces, which when their presence is first discerned by him, appear as rootless vectors, volatile, mimetic, ephemeral. And even should he overcome his fear, the assimilation of these forces, by which, acknowledged or not, his life is determined, does not appeal to him.

In one story the agent follows the girl across the fields while the soldiers in the barracks snore drunkenly. She looks back at him with only the light of the stars between them, and the look she gives, whether fear or desire on her part or neither or both, is a beckoning. She disappears into the dark of the jungle beyond.

He follows.

In a clearing he comes across a fire and she is sitting by it looking up at him, expecting, waiting.

He wants to ask, Why did I follow you? but he doesn't.

She just sits there, her eyes holding the light of the fire, her skin its warmth.

In this story she feeds him from a pail suspended from an iron tripod over the flames. It is the intestines of some animal and at first he is hesitant, but she extends her hand out toward him as he holds the bowl before him and she makes an innocent encouraging gesture to eat. He does. It is hot and the flavor he remembers as something from his childhood, something he had forgotten until now.

When he is done she stands up and reaches her hand out to him. He rises and takes it and it is small and soft in his. She leads him through the trees, through the bushes. It is pitch black away from the fire and he follows as a blind man, his steps short and tentative upon the uneven ground, his trust in her, out of necessity, complete. Just at the moment when he sees a pale light coming through the foliage ahead, the girl drops his hand and goes quickly forward. He sees her silhouette move into the light and he follows and they step one after the other from the dense leafy wall of jungle and stand in the starlight on the bank of a large pond.

The girl pulls her rough dress up over her head and stands naked before him and he can see her dark skin, her small breasts with slightly upturned nipples protruding gracefully from her slender chest.

She reaches up and pushes something into his mouth. It tastes sweet, flowery, some fruit which he has never before experienced. Then he watches as she steps into the water and drops with a light splash and swims out into the dark.

There are many stories about what happens next. They all begin with him taking off his clothes and stepping in after her.

In another story, one that also happened and which also delivered him, he is standing for a moment in that starlit field, the plowed furrows running away from him on all sides, her eyes meeting his where she has stopped and turned at the edge of the jungle with a look he could discern but not interpret. He wondered should he turn around and go back. It was a rare moment in his life, he suddenly realized, when all things hung in the balance. He had never experienced such a moment, and though he did not know who was the judge of such weights and measures, he knew at that moment that the scale had been set.

The girl disappeared into the darkness of the trees.

He went after her.

The dark of the undergrowth was so thick that he didn't see the light of the fire until he'd almost stepped into it. Seeing the girl sitting beside a man with a large out-of-date carbine resting across his knees, he knew instantly. And the next instant he felt the hard sharp butt of a rifle slam against his head and he slumped to the ground.

Acknowledgments

This story originally appeared in *Oyster Boy Review*, Winter 2003–2004.

Matthew Raymond teaches English in California. His stories have appeared in *Oyster Boy Review* and *Euphony*. His poems have appeared in *Parcel, Beloit Poetry Journal, Permafrost, Grasslands,* and *Sulphur River Literary Review. The Muddy Season* is his first chapbook.